Before reading

Look at the book cov
Ask, "What do you thi

To build independen   d
at the start of this book. If the child needs help, turn
back to pages 6 and 7 in **2a** and read the words again with
the child.

During reading

Offer plenty of support and praise as the child reads the story.
Listen carefully and respond to events in the text.

In **2c**, the new **Key Words** are not shown at the bottom of
the page. If the child hesitates over a word, turn to the back
of the book to practise reading it together. If the word is
phonically decodable, you can sound out the letters and
blend the sounds to read the word ("d-o-g, dog"). Praise the
child for their effort, then return to the story.

Pause every few pages and ask questions to check the child's
understanding of what they have read. If they begin to lose
concentration, stop reading and save the page for later.

Celebrate the child's achievement and come back to the
story the next day.

After reading

After reading this book, ask, "Did you enjoy the story? What did
you like about it?" Encourage the child to share their opinions.

Use the comprehension questions on page 54 to check the
child's understanding and recall of the text.

Ladybird

Series Consultant: Professor David Waugh
With thanks to Kulwinder Maude

LADYBIRD BOOKS

UK | USA | Canada | Ireland | Australia
India | New Zealand | South Africa

Ladybird Books is part of the Penguin Random House group of companies
whose addresses can be found at global.penguinrandomhouse.com.
www.penguin.co.uk   www.puffin.co.uk   www.ladybird.co.uk

Original edition of Key Words with Peter and Jane first published by Ladybird Books Ltd 1964
Series updated 2023
This book first published 2023
001

Text copyright © Ladybird Books Ltd, 1964, 2023
Illustrations by Nuno Alexandre Vieira
Based on characters and design by Gustavo Mazali
Illustrations copyright © Ladybird Books Ltd, 2023

With thanks to Liz Pemberton for her contributions in advising on the illustrations
With thanks to Inclusive Minds for connecting us with their Inclusion Ambassador network,
and in particular thanks to Guntaas Kaur Chugh for her input on the illustrations

Printed in China

The authorized representative in the EEA is Penguin Random House Ireland,
Morrison Chambers, 32 Nassau Street, Dublin D02 YH68

A CIP catalogue record for this book is available from the British Library

ISBN: 978-0-241-51078-0

All correspondence to:
Ladybird Books
Penguin Random House Children's
One Embassy Gardens, 8 Viaduct Gardens, London SW11 7BW

MIX
Paper from
responsible sources
FSC® C018179

Key Words

with Peter and Jane

2c

Fun in the water

Based on the original
Key Words with Peter and Jane
reading scheme and research by William Murray

Original edition written by William Murray
This edition written by Zoë Clarke
Illustrated by Nuno Alexandre Vieira
Based on characters and design by Gustavo Mazali

Peter and Jane are
in the water.

They can have fun
in the water.

Look! It is Tess.

She is in the water.

She has fun.

They have a ball.

"Tess wants it,"
Jane says.

"Come on! Jump, jump!" Peter says.

They jump.

Tess jumps.

Can you jump?

"Look! Fish!"
Peter says.

They look. It is a fish!

"Look! The fish can jump!" Jane says.

"Come on. Look, look!" she says.

Peter comes and looks.

Tess wants the fish.

Tess jumps in the water.

"Look! The tree is in the water," Peter says.

"Can you jump on the tree? It looks fun," Jane says.

"I can! I can! I can
have fun on it,"
says Peter.

"Come on, Tess!
You are on it,"
Jane says.

Jane jumps in
the water.

"I want the ball,"
she says.

Peter jumps in the water.

"I want it!" Peter says.

"You can have it,"
Jane says.

Tess is in the water.

She wants the ball.

"You can have it!
Come on!" Peter
says.

"I want water,"
Jane says.

The shop has water.

"It's a fish! Can I have a fish?" says Peter.

"You can have a fish," Jane says.

She has a fish.

They have fish.

They have water.

"It's fun here!"
they say.

Questions

Answer these questions about the story.

1 Who jumps in the water with Peter and Jane?

2 What do Peter and Jane see in the water?

3 What do they get at the shop?